ANDY SHANE
Is NOT in Love

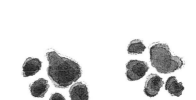

ANDY SHANE
Is NOT in Love

Jennifer Richard Jacobson
illustrated by Abby Carter

CANDLEWICK PRESS
CAMBRIDGE, MASSACHUSETTS

For Jackie, Mary, and Dana — with love
J. R. J.

To Doug, Samantha, Carter, and Duffy
A. C.

Text copyright © 2008 by Jennifer Richard Jacobson
Illustrations copyright © 2008 by Abby Carter

First edition 2008

Library of Congress Cataloging-in-Publication Data

Jacobson, Jennifer, date.
Andy Shane is NOT in love / Jennifer Richard Jacobson ; illustrated by Abby Carter. —1st ed.
p. cm.
Summary: When Andy Shane befriends the new girl in town, everyone thinks he must be in love with her,
but the reason he is spending so much time with her is because her dog just had puppies.
ISBN 978-0-7636-3212-0
[1. Dogs—Fiction. 2. Animals—Infancy—Fiction. 3. Friendship—Fiction.]
I. Carter, Abby, ill. II. Title.
PZ7.J1529 Ani 2008
[E]—dc22   2007052880

2 4 6 8 10 9 7 5 3 1

Printed in the United States of America

This book was typeset in Vendome.
The illustrations were done in black pencil and black watercolor wash.

Candlewick Press
2067 Massachusetts Avenue
Cambridge, Massachusetts 02140

visit us at www.candlewick.com

CONTENTS

1

New Girl in Town

Dolores Starbuckle leaned over Andy Shane's desk. She pointed to the picture Andy was drawing. "Make a turret here," she said.

"What's a turret?" asked Yumi.

"It's the pointy part of a castle," said Dolores.

"Who said we're making a castle?" asked Andy. He and Dolores were busy planning the snow fort they would make when the snow was warm enough and wet enough to stick.

"Good morning, class," said Ms. Janice.

"Good morning, Ms. Janice," said the students, looking up from their books and games and papers.

Ms. Janice was not alone. She had her arm around a girl who was wearing pink overalls and lime-green sneakers tied with ribbons instead of shoelaces. The girl's eyes seemed to dance.

"This is Lark Alice Bell," said Ms.

Janice. "She's just moved to town and

will be in our class this year."

"Hello, Lark," said Dolores,

shooting her hand into the air. "I'll be

your helper if you want. I know all the

class rules and procedures, such as,

'Be responsible and respectful.'"

"Thank you, Dolores," said Ms. Janice. "Perhaps you can be Lark's guide on the playground. I thought Andy Shane might like to help Lark in class this morning."

"Lucky duck," whispered Dolores.

"Andy, please come forward and meet Lark," said Ms. Janice.

Andy's face turned the color of his favorite crayon: Razzle Dazzle Rose.

"Oooh," said the other kids.

Andy showed Lark where to sit

during morning meeting,

where to find the math materials,

and where to sharpen her pencil.

At recess, Dolores made it clear

that it was *her* turn to be the helper.

So Andy ran off to climb the big

snowbank left by the plow.

He dug a hole and sat in the bottom.

It was a peaceful place to be.

"Hi, Andy Shane," said a voice from the top of his hole. "What are you *doing* in there?"

"Just sitting," said Andy. "Come on down."

Lark slipped in next to Andy. "This is like a cave," she said.

Andy smiled. He was proud of his hole.

"The closet in my old house felt like a cave," said Lark. "That's where my dog had her puppies."

"You have puppies?" asked Andy.

"Four," said Lark. "They're yellow Lab puppies. They're so cute. They have these little bodies with giant paws and big noses."

"I have wanted a dog my whole life," said Andy. "My Granny Webb said *maybe* I was old enough to get one."

"Does 'maybe' mean yes, or does 'maybe' mean no?"

"With Granny Webb, 'maybe' means 'maybe,'" said Andy.

"*Maybe*," said Lark, "you can have one of mine."

2

First Comes Love

"There you are, Lark!" said Dolores, peering down the hole. "I've been looking everywhere for you! The bell already rang!"

"It did? Oh, no!" said Andy. "We have to go!"

Lark and Andy squirmed up out of the snow cave and ran as fast as they could. They reached the end of the line just as the last of the children were entering the building.

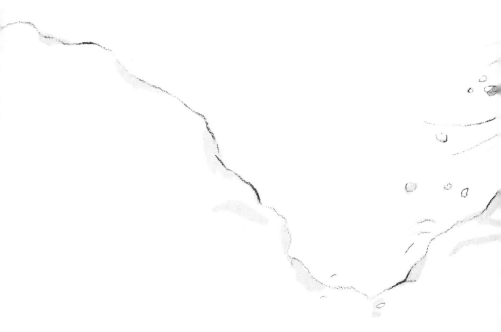

"Hurry up, Andy! Hurry up, Lark!"

called Dolores from inside the door.

Big kids were standing in the hall waiting for their turn at the water fountain. One started singing, "Andy and Lark sitting in a tree, K-I-S-S-I-N-G!"

Andy Shane stopped. He put his shoulders back. He stared at those kids. He didn't move a muscle.

One boy laughed nervously.

"Come on, Lark," said Andy.

"You are not being responsible and

respectful!" Dolores told the big kids.

Without even taking her snowsuit off, Dolores marched right over to Andy's desk. "For your information, *I* was supposed to be Lark's helper at recess."

But Andy wasn't ready to listen. He was writing down his name and phone number for Lark. Lark wrote down her name and phone number for Andy.

"Do you want *my* phone number?" Dolores asked Lark, but Lark just looked confused.

"Today you will need a reading

buddy," said Ms. Janice.

Lark reached out and grabbed

Andy's hand.

That startled Andy. He and Dolores

had always been reading buddies. But

Andy *was* supposed to be Lark's helper.

He looked at Dolores and shrugged.

Dolores just turned and walked away.

While Ms. Janice reminded them of the jobs of reading buddies, Andy Shane doodled on the back of his notebook. He made a big heart and wrote LAB inside.

Dolores, who was supposed to be reading with Polly, leaned way over in her seat to see what Andy was writing.

Andy tried to cover it with his hand, but Dolores had already seen.

"L-A-B," she whispered loudly. "That stands for *Lark Alice Bell.* Why, you *are* in love, Andy Shane!"

Then she fell out of her seat onto the floor.

3

Hurt Feelings

On Saturday, Lark came to Andy's house.

"Why, Lark, I've heard so much about you," said Granny Webb.

She made them cocoa with marsh-mallows. "Now tell me about the puppies."

Lark told Granny that all of the puppies had been spoken for except one. "He is the most playful puppy of all," said Lark. "If you give him a carrot top, he'll chase it across the floor like it's a bug or a mouse."

"I guess we'd better start saving our carrot tops," said Granny.

Andy jumped up and wrapped his arms around Granny. "You'll see, Granny. I'll take really good care of this puppy."

"We'll have to think of a name," said Granny Webb.

When they finished their cocoa,
Andy and Lark put on their winter
gear and headed outside.

"This is the field behind my house,"
said Andy.

"Dogs love to run in fields," said Lark.

"And these are my woods," said Andy.

"Dogs love to sniff in woods,"
said Lark.

"And this is my sledding hill,"
said Andy.

"*I* love to sled!" said Lark.

Andy got his flying saucer, and he
and Lark slid down the hill over and
over again.

"Hey," said Lark, "want to build a snow fort?"

There was nothing Andy loved more in winter than building snow forts. He and Lark scooped up the perfectly sticky snow and piled it high.

Then they crawled inside. They made two little seats, a table, and a shelf.

Andy recognized that voice. That voice belonged to another person who loved to build snow forts—someone who had planned all year with Andy to make the coolest fort ever, someone who was waiting for Andy to call and say, "The snow is ready! Come now!"

"Dolores!" said Andy, jumping out
of the fort.

"I was waiting for you to call, Andy.
The snow is perfect."

"I forgot, but look," he said,

stepping back and pointing to his fort.

"Isn't it cool?"

"Wow! It *is* cool. Did you do this all

by yourself?" asked Dolores.

Two snowflake mittens appeared

from the fort. Lark popped out.

Andy felt terrible. He hadn't meant to build a fort without Dolores. And now it looked as if he'd had a fort party and she wasn't invited.

"Want to help us put the roof on?" asked Andy.

"I thought you were my best friend, Andy Shane," said Dolores, crossing her arms over her chest. "I can't believe you and Lark built this fort without me! That is so mean!"

Dolores turned and stomped back
to the driveway. She nearly bumped
into Granny Webb, who was carrying
a soup pot.

"What's the matter, Dolores?"

asked Granny.

"She's mad because *we* were

supposed to make a fort today," said

Andy, running over.

"Oh, I see," said Granny. She reached down and took Dolores's hand. "I think it's time we all met Andy's new best friend," she said.

4

Things Are Not Always as They Seem

"I am not in the mood for any more new friends," said Dolores as Lark led the way up the hill to her new house.

"Especially when they cause your old friends to treat you shabbily."

When they arrived, Granny Webb handed Lark's mother the pot of soup. "Welcome to the neighborhood," she said.

Lark's mother started telling Granny all about the move. She seemed really happy to have a new friend.

Lark led Dolores and Andy down-

stairs to the basement.

"You know, I did have plans of my

own this afternoon," said Dolores.

"I don't need to be

following you around.

I am sure there are lots of people who would like to be my friend."

"Dolores, you've got it all wrong," said Andy.

Dolores's voice just got louder. "People who wouldn't desert me on the playground. People who would be my reading buddy. People who would like to build a snow fort with me."

Lark brought them to a large box.

"Oooh," said Dolores, reaching in.
"Puppies!"

"Which one is mine?"
asked Andy.

Lark pointed to the one trying to climb the sides of the box. Every time he stretched, he flipped over. "That one," she said, laughing.

"Yours?" asked Dolores.

"Yup," said Andy, picking up the pup and holding him to his cheek. "Granny said I could have one."

"You lucky duck!" said Dolores, patting the puppy in Andy's arms. "What kind of dog is he?"

"He's a Lab," said Lark.

"A Lab?" said Dolores. "L-A-B?
Oh!" Now her face was the color of
Razzle Dazzle Rose.

"Granny Webb was right," said
Dolores. "You do have a new best
friend, Andy."

Lark sighed. "I miss *my* best friends," she said.

"But you have us!" said Dolores, putting her arm around Lark. "Andy and I will be your new best friends."

"And Lucky Duck, too!" said
Andy, holding up his puppy.

"You can't call a dog a duck," said
Dolores.

"I can if I want to," said Andy.
"Right, Lucky Duck?" He gave his
dog a big squeeze. Lucky Duck licked
Andy's face.

"Andy Shane's in love," said Dolores.

But this time, no one seemed to mind.